Katie Morag
and the Grand Concert

High Farm

The Holiday House

Mrs Bayview's

The Lady Artist's

The Redburn Bridge

The Village

Nurse's

Effie
&
Ronald
the
Road's

Mrs
Baxter's

Neilly
Beag's

The
Ferryman's

TEAS

For all Prima Donnas

KATIE MORAG AND THE GRAND CONCERT
A RED FOX BOOK 978 1 849 41087 8

First published in Great Britain by The Bodley Head,
an imprint of Random House Children's Books
A Random House Group Company

Bodley Head edition published 1997
Red Fox edition published 1999
This Red Fox edition published 2010

1 3 5 7 9 10 8 6 4 2

Copyright © Mairi Hedderwick, 1997

The right of Mairi Hedderwick to be identified as the author and illustrator of this work has
been asserted in accordance with the Copyright, Designs and Patents Act 1988.

Red Fox Books are published by Random House Children's Books,
61–63 Uxbridge Road, London W5 5SA

www.**kids**at**random**house.co.uk
www.**rbooks**.co.uk

Addresses for companies within The Random House Group Limited can be found at:
www.randomhouse.co.uk/offices.htm

THE RANDOM HOUSE GROUP Limited Reg. No. 954009

A CIP catalogue record for this book is available from the British Library.

Printed in China

Katie Morag
and the Grand Concert

Mairi Hedderwick

ISLE of STRUAY

Programme

SVEN & SEAN OLSEN

KATIE MORAG McCOLL

HEVVIE BEVVIE BAND

in aid of

GRAND CONCERT

GERTRUDE ISOBEL

BOG COTTON REEL BAND

NEILLY BEAG

Struay Music Society

RED FOX

Once in a while on the Isle of Struay there is a Grand Concert.

Everyone who can, practises songs and dances, poems, fiddle and pipe tunes for months in advance.

This concert was going to be extra grand; Katie Morag McColl's uncles Sven and Sean were coming. They were world famous musicians. And they were twins. Everyone practised harder than usual for the special occasion.

Katie Morag asked if she could sing at the Grand Concert.

"Yes! Yes!" answered Mrs McColl impatiently. Liam was missing and the baby had just woken up. "What song?" asked Mr McColl, who was equally preoccupied with stacking shelves.

"I don't know," replied Katie Morag, tearfully.

"Now don't YOU start crying!" shouted Mrs McColl.

"Grannie Island will teach you a song," soothed Mr McColl.

"You'll have to practise every day, remember..." added Mrs McColl.

THOUGHT FOR THE DAY

DON'T SWEAT THE SMALL STUFF — IT'S ALL SMALL STUFF

M.V. STRUAY LASS

WILD LIFE CRUISES

CONTACT: GUY, THE FERRYMAN'S HOUSE (in the VILLAGE)

WEATHER PERMITTING

GRAND CONCERT

ARTISTES

ISLE OF STRUAY SHOP

On the long walk over to Grannie Island's Katie Morag began to wonder if
it was such a good idea to perform at the Concert. Suddenly she felt very shy.

"Are you singing at the Grand Concert?" she asked Agnes.

"Oh no!" replied Agnes. "I don't like singing. I like clapping
as loud as I can in the audience. I'm going to wear my new dress."

Katie Morag felt even worse.

Grannie Island said she had sung – and danced – with the best in her younger days. "Though nobody would believe that now..." she sighed.

"I do!" said Katie Morag.

Grannie Island got down her fiddle and played 'Ho Ro My Nut Brown Maiden' and 'I Know Where I Am Going' and 'You Cannae Shove Your Granny Off a Bus'. Katie Morag liked the last one best. She soon learned the words which were a bit naughty.

That night in bed Katie Morag fell asleep listening to Grannie Island softly singing Uncle Sven's favourite song; all about a lovely garden and a lady called Maude. Katie Morag wondered if Maude had a pretty new dress.

THE
SONG OF THE
GRANDMOTHERS

O YOU CANN—AE SHOVE YOUR GRA—NNY OFF A BUS, O YOU CANN—AE SHOVE YOUR GRA—NNY OFF A BUS, O YOU CANN—AE SHOVE YOUR GRA—NNY, FOR SHE'S YOUR MA—MMY'S MA—MMY, YOU CANN—AE SHOVE YOUR GRA—NNY OFF A BUS.

YOU CAN SHOVE YOUR OTHER GRANNY OFF A BUS,
YOU CAN SHOVE YOUR OTHER GRANNY OFF A BUS,
YOU CAN SHOVE YOUR OTHER GRANNY,
FOR SHE'S YOUR DADDY'S MAMMY!
YOU CAN SHOVE YOUR OTHER GRANNY OFF A BUS!

When Uncle Sven and Uncle Sean arrived Katie Morag could not work out which uncle was which. They were absolutely identical.

"Hello, Katie Morag!" smiled Sven.

"Hiya, Matie Korag!" smiled Sean.

They had brought lots of presents and an extra one for Katie Morag from Granma Mainland who lived in the faraway city.

Inside the box was the most beautiful dress that Katie Morag had ever seen.
"Come and have some parsnip soup after your long journey!"
called Mrs McColl. Sven had two helpings, Sean had three.
"Delicious!" said Sven.
"Fabbydoo!" said Sean.

After supper Uncle Sven and Uncle Sean said they would like to practise for the concert. Katie Morag said she would too and was allowed to stand on the table to sing her song.

When it got to the bit, "You can shove your OTHER granny off a bus" everyone laughed.

But Katie Morag knew she wouldn't ever do such a thing to either of her grandmothers. It was just a joke. She loved them both too much.

"Well done!" cheered Uncle Sven.

"Right Bobby Dazzling!" cheered Uncle Sean.

It was going to be a WONDERFUL concert, thought Katie Morag.

: Katie Morag McColl
: Granma Mainland

"Goodnight, sleep well," yawned Uncle Sven when it was time for bed.

"Tattie bye, peepers sleepers," yawned Uncle Sean.

"Where is Liam!" worried Mrs McColl.

Liam was nowhere to be seen.

He was not behind the couch, nor under the table; he was not in the loo nor inside the biscuit cupboard; he was not in his bed.

"The door!" cried Katie Morag. It was wide open...

ISLE of STRUAY YOU ARE HERE

Everyone went shouting out into the night, waving torches.
"Liam! Liam! Where are you? Come here! Come here!"
Uncle Sven shouted the loudest and longest.
Mrs McColl was quite distraught. "He's in the sea!" she screamed.
All the lights and shouting woke Liam up.

Liam nearly wasn't allowed to go to the Concert after causing so much trouble. Mrs McColl relented at the last minute.

Katie Morag peeped through the curtains. She was so excited! The dress fitted perfectly and look! Granma Mainland had caught the second boat. There she was sitting in the front row looking so pretty. Liam was beside her, holding her hand.

Everything was perfect.

And then Katie Morag saw Agnes. She was also sitting in the front row. And she was wearing the EXACT SAME DRESS...

No one was ever, ever as miserable as Katie Morag was at that precise moment. She ran off backstage, big tears filling her eyes.

"I'm not singing!" she wailed at Grannie Island.

And there was Uncle Sven with big tears in his eyes, too. "I've lost my voice," he croaked.

Grannie Island tried to comfort them both, her own eyes glistening. The Concert was a disaster before it had even started.

It was a terrible thing to see grown ups with tears in their eyes, thought Katie Morag, as she rubbed her own dry.

"Come on, Uncle Sean. I'll sing Uncle Sven's song for him."

Grannie Island gave Sven a hankie and then her fiddle. "You don't need a voice for this," she encouraged, pushing him onto the stage behind Katie Morag and Uncle Sean.

The trio gave the performance of their lives. The audience went wild. Agnes clapped until her hands were sore.

The Grand Concert was off to a very grand start!

Katie Morag did not mind not singing the Granny song. It would not be so very funny with the two grandmothers listening, would it?

At the end of the night there was a party in the Village Hall. All the islanders wanted Sven and Sean's autographs. "Do you know which is Sven and which is Sean?" they whispered.

Katie Morag and Agnes had their own party up on the stage. They had so enjoyed being twins they decided to wear the same clothes one day a week from now on – and confuse everybody.

Do you know which one is Katie Morag and which is Agnes?

"I do!" said Uncle Sven.

And Uncle Sean said, "Fabbydoolidoozie, so do I!"

TEAS

Join Katie Morag on more adventures!

Katie Morag and the Big Boy Cousins

Katie Morag Delivers the Mail

Katie Morag and the Riddles

Katie Morag and the Wedding

Katie Morag and the Birthdays

Katie Morag and the Tiresome Ted

Katie Morag and the Two Grandmothers

Katie Morag and the Dancing Class

Katie Morag and the New Pier

Katie Morag's Island Stories

More Katie Morag Island Stories

The Big Katie Morag Storybook

The Second Katie Morag Storybook